KINDERKITTENS

Who Took the Cookie from the Cookie Jar?

by Stephanie Calmenson
Illustrated by Diane deGroat

Cartwheel
·B·O·O·K·S· ®

Scholastic Inc.
New York Toronto London Auckland Sydney

To Gloria Bardin
— S.C.

ISBN 0-590-46350-0

Text copyright © 1995 by Stephanie Calmenson.
Illustrations copyright © 1995 by Diane deGroat.
All rights reserved. Published by Scholastic Inc.
CARTWHEEL BOOKS is a registered trademark of Scholastic Inc.

12 11 10 9 8 7 6 5 4 3 2 1   5 6 7 8 9/9 0/0

Printed in the U.S.A.   24

First Scholastic printing, April 1995

It was a busy morning in Ms. Calico's kindergarten class. The Kinderkittens were all doing interesting things.

Sophie and Cosmo were building a tower with blocks.

Stanley was reading a good book.

And Nikki was in the Math Corner counting and sorting beads.

Clap! Clap! Clap!
The Kinderkittens knew what it meant when Ms. Calico clapped three times. They stopped what they were doing and sang:

We had fun at work and play.
It's cleanup time — put things away!

They put away blocks and books, beads and buttons. They washed paintbrushes and hung up paintings to dry.

When the room was neat and clean, the Kinderkittens gathered around Ms. Calico at the piano.

"Who would like to play The Cookie Jar Game?" asked Ms. Calico.

"Me! Me! Me!" cried the Kinderkittens.

It was Stanley's turn to go first. The class tapped their paws on the floor as Stanley chanted, *"Who took the cookie from the cookie jar?"*

Stanley pointed to Sophie and said,
"Sophie took the cookie from the cookie jar!"
Sophie popped up and cried, *"Who me?"*
"Yes, you!" answered Stanley.
"Couldn't be!" said Sophie.
"Then who?" asked Stanley.

Sophie pointed to Nikki.
"*Nikki took the cookie from the cookie jar!*"
"*Who me?*" answered Nikki, jumping up.
"*Yes, you!*" laughed Sophie.

"*Couldn't be!*" said Nikki.
"*Then who?*" asked Sophie.

Nikki pointed to Cosmo and began to sing, "*Cosmo took the cookie from the cookie jar!*"

Before Cosmo had a chance to answer, there was a knock on the door. The Kinderkittens turned around and saw Mr. Pawpaw, the school principal, standing in the doorway.

"Good morning, everyone," said
Mr. Pawpaw. "How are you today?"
"Fine!" answered the Kinderkittens
all together. "How are you?"
"Very well, thank you," said Mr.
Pawpaw. "Don't let me interrupt you.
I was just passing by and wanted to
say hello."
The Kinderkittens played their
game, while Mr. Pawpaw walked around
the room admiring their wonderful
artwork. Then he waved good-bye.

"It's time for our snack now," said Ms. Calico. "Nikki, I noticed you were counting and matching in the Math Corner this morning. Would you like to count out cookies for the class today?"

"Yes!" said Nikki. She washed her paws, then counted out one plate for every kitten in the room and one for Ms. Calico.

Next, she counted out two cookies for each plate. But when she got to the last plate, there was only one cookie left in the jar.

"Ms. Calico! Ms. Calico!" called Nikki. "Someone took a cookie from the cookie jar!"

"Oh, Nikki. Our game is over. It's snack time now," said Ms. Calico.

"No, really! There is only one cookie left. There should be two," explained Nikki.

"Hmm. That is strange," said Ms. Calico. "I counted the cookies when I came in this morning."

"That means someone took one!" called Stanley. "I am a good detective. I will find out who took the cookie from the cookie jar!"

He got a magnifying glass from the Science Corner and searched the room.

Stanley was still looking for the cookie when Sophie popped up and said, "I am a good detective, too! I will check the cubbies."

Soon all the Kinderkittens were searching for the missing cookie. But they could not find it anywhere.

"Oh, well. I must have counted wrong. Everyone makes mistakes. Even teachers," said Ms. Calico. "Today I will have one cookie instead of two. And tomorrow, we can bake cookies together. We will make extra cookies, too. That way we'll be sure there are plenty to go around."

"Hurray!" shouted the Kinderkittens.

The next morning, Ms. Calico brought in all the ingredients they needed to bake cookies.

There was lots to do. The Kinderkittens took turns pouring and mixing and measuring.

Then Ms. Calico put the cookies into the oven.

While the cookies were baking, the Kinderkittens played The Cookie Jar Game. This time Sophie went first. The Kinderkittens began tapping on the floor as Sophie chanted, *"Who took the cookie from the cookie jar?"*

Sophie stood up and pointed to Ms. Calico.

"Ms. Calico took the cookie from the cookie jar!"

Ms. Calico smiled and said, *"Who me?"*

"Yes, you!" giggled Sophie.

"Couldn't be!" said Ms. Calico.

"Then who?" asked Sophie.

Just then, Mr. Pawpaw popped his head in the door and sang, *"Oh, I took the cookie from the cookie jar!"*

He walked into the room and explained. "I took a cookie yesterday when I was visiting. I forgot to say thank you."

"You took the cookie?" asked Stanley. He picked up the magnifying glass and raced over to Mr. Pawpaw.

"Yes, I think I see a cookie crumb," Stanley said.

Mr. Pawpaw sniffed the air and smiled. The good smell of cookies baking filled the room.

"Won't you join us for snack today?" asked Ms. Calico. "We have plenty of cookies to share."

"Why, thank you," said Mr. Pawpaw.
"I get hungry just about this time every
morning. And I do love cookies!"

Mr. Pawpaw pulled up a chair and bit into a cookie that was still warm from the oven.

"Mmm," he said. "Kinderkitten cookies are the best!"

From that day on, Mr. Pawpaw joined the class for snack whenever he could. And on days when he was too busy to come to the classroom, the Kinderkittens took turns delivering a snack to his office.

The Kinderkittens even made up a new
ending for "The Cookie Jar Song." Whenever they
finished playing the game, they all sang together:
Who took the cookie from the cookie jar?
Mr. Pawpaw took the cookie from the cookie jar!
Would you like a cookie? Please be our guest.
Kinderkitten cookies are the best!

The Kinderkitten
Cookie Jar Song

Who took the cook-ie from the cook-ie jar? Mis-ter

Paw-paw took the cook-ie from the cook-ie jar!

Would you like a cook-ie? Please be our guest.

Kin-der-kit-ten cook-ies are the best!

Mmm...

COUNT AND MATCH

Feed the Kinderkittens! Count the number
of cookies on each plate below. Then count the
number of kittens at each table on the next page.
Point to each plate of cookies. Then point to the
table with the same number of Kinderkittens.

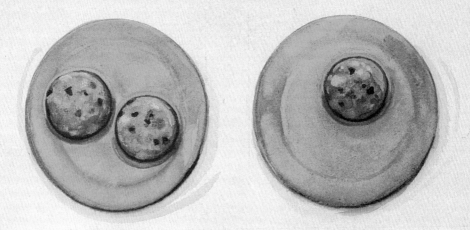

KINDERKITTEN COOKIE RECIPE

Always be a careful Kinderkitten. Never touch an oven by yourself. Ask a grown-up to help you make these delicious oatmeal-raisin cookies.

What You Need:

1 cup unsifted flour
1 teaspoon baking soda
¾ cup margarine or butter
½ cup sugar
½ cup firmly packed brown sugar
1 egg
1 teaspoon vanilla
1 ¾ cups uncooked oats
1 cup raisins

What to Do:

1. In a mixing bowl, mix together the flour and baking soda.
2. In a larger bowl, blend the margarine, sugars, egg, and vanilla.
3. Add the flour mixture and mix well.
4. Stir in the oats and raisins.
5. Drop the batter by teaspoons onto an ungreased cookie sheet.
6. Bake at 375° for 10 to 12 minutes or until cookies are light brown.
7. Remove the cookies with a spatula and place on a rack to cool.
8. Enjoy!